I0618234

SILENT MARS

AND OTHER STORIES

SILENT MARS

AND OTHER STORIES

PAUL V. CWIAKALA

Silk Baron Independent Press
Paterson, New Jersey

This is a work of fiction. Names, characters, businesses, places, events
and incidents are either the products of the author's imagination or
used in a fictitious manner. Any resemblance to actual persons, living
or dead, or actual events is purely coincidental.

Cover Image retrieved from Pixabay.com, May 2016. The Image is a
Public Domain work and its use here is within the terms of the Creative
Commons CC0 1.0 Universal License.

Cover design by Silk Baron Independent Press
Book design and production by Silk Baron Independent Press
Editing by Silk Baron Independent Press

Silk Baron Independent Press
www.silkbaronindependentpress.com

Table of Contents

Silent Mars

Raniero Alba, startled by the blast, stumbled as the plume of sand erupted into the Martian sky. Until a few moments ago, he'd been examining pebbles for evidence of water erosion as part of his geological survey of Mare Platia.

"What was that?"

He regained his footing and wiped rusted sand from his spacesuit's visor.

"No clue," Kemal Mitamar, Raniero's survey partner, said as he shut off his spectrometer. "It was close, though, less than a mile away."

Finished gawking, Raniero trotted back to their truck – a rough heavy-duty machine based on a military model – and tapped into the onboard radio.

"Team Four to Jamestown, do you copy? We just witnessed a very large explosion, about twenty minutes out from you, over," he said.

"Jamestown to Team Four. We felt it, Raniero. How close were you?"

"It was a mile to the west of us, maybe less than that. Do you want us to investigate?"

There was quiet, and then the shuffling of a microphone changing hands.

"Team Four, this is Commander Garcia. I want you to investigate, but be cautious. Assume it was a meteor impact, but return to base immediately if it looks to have destabilized the ground. Team Seven reported that there might be dried lava tubes underground in that area."

"Understood. We'll report as soon as we've found the crater."

"We're repositioning a satellite now to get a better look as soon as the dust clears."

"Understood, over and out."

Raniero turned to Kemal again, a gloomy pink haze suffocating everything. In a few moments, he was enveloped by the dust cloud and couldn't see his own hand if stretched out at arm's length. He activated his helmet lights and flipped through vision settings: thermal, infrared, radiological, and a few others.

"Wow, my vision degraded really fast. I can't see anything."

"Yeah," Kemal replied. "Are you detecting any heat or radiation?"

"No."

Kemal stepped away from the truck and vanished into the haze. Was it Raniero's imagination or could it be getting worse? It couldn't be a sandstorm, it was the wrong time of year for that and Jamestown would have warned them if there was a freak one on the way.

"Hey, Kemal, come back here. I can't see you anymore," Raniero said.

There was no response.

"Kemal? Can you hear me?"

Static.

Raniero switched to techlepathy – direct brain-to-brain radio communication – and called Kemal via his personal wi-fi implant, but again there was no response. Raniero couldn't even feel Dr. Mitamar's presence anymore.

He'd never felt so alone.

He tried to control his breathing.

"Team Four to Jamestown," he said. "Conditions are worse than expected and I have lost Mitamar. Please advise."

No response.

He was about to turn back to the truck and try again when a sound, definitely a voice, whispered itself into his mind through his radio implant.

"Kemal?" he said.

The sound came again, too faint to make out, although he was sure that the word spoken was "Raniero". Was Kemal calling out to him? Perhaps the meteor itself was jamming the signal…could it be emitting radiation or electro-magnetic waves? If that were the case, then why didn't he detect anything like that? Raniero walked in the direction Kemal had vanished.

He was being watched. He could sense it, that innate intuition that screams when eyes are focused on you. They were unfriendly eyes.

It wasn't a new feeling for anyone on Mars: along with the unnerving dreams, everybody was spooked by the sheer loneliness of the world. When he was younger, much younger, he would've chalked it up to ghosts. Superstitious visitors to the Red Planet thought it was haunted by the extinct civilization of ancient Mars, but Mars is dead – not just dead, but never lived in the first place. A lifeless, rusted peroxide desert. This fact has been established for two hundred years, though the myth of the Martians persevered regardless. It was kind of funny actually. Ghostly Martians? Even if Martians had existed, it wasn't likely they'd have ghosts. Ghosts aren't real anyway.

The feeling subsided and Raniero decided to forget it.

He reached the edge of the crater. With a single thought, he set his implant to record his spoken words and save them to the Flash Drive connected to the space suit.

"I have found the crater," he said. "Visibility is very low and I'm unable to make out much detail."

He crouched and examined the shattered soil and stone.

"Based on initial visual analysis, I am going to estimate that the meteorite was traveling from a northerly direction and at incredible speed," he said. "Also, based on what little curve I can see, I am also going to guess that the diameter of the crater is between twenty and sixty meters. All of this will need to be verified at a later date... a full reconnaissance team should be dispatched to this location at the next opportunity."

Carefully, Raniero stepped into the crater itself.

Ahead, through the mist, he could make out a faint glow. Was it Kemal?

No.

But, if it were the meteorite, an unlikelihood in and of itself, wouldn't his thermometer be detecting the heat?

"I can see a yellow or orange light through the dust," he said. "I believe it may be the meteorite, although I cannot yet explain the cause of the light emission. I'm going to take a closer look."

As Raniero approached, the light intensified, threatening to overwhelm his visor's filters and blind him.

Suddenly the haze cleared, as if Raniero had stepped out of the cloud entirely.

"O-okay... I have... apparently, stepped into some kind of air pocket...within the dust cloud," he said. "It's bright enough see without my lights, although there is no sunlight penetrating the dust. The light appears to be internally produced by..."

...A Faberge egg?

It was golden, polished to a mirrored shine, and resembled a large, ornately decorated egg. Its surface was encrusted in gems, emeralds and rubies, and two pairs of spindly legs stabbed into the charred soil beneath it. Two rings encircled these legs: one made of a clear crystal, the other a duller material. The light seemed more to shine on the egg than be its source, though that made less sense than the egg's existence.

Was he hallucinating? He reached, slow and halting, and touched the egg. Suddenly, it flashed at Raniero, who shouted and stumbled backward. In that moment, Dr. Alba at once became aware of... another. There was a presence with him, surrounding him, engulfing him... within him.

- - -

Panicked and disoriented, Raniero rolled over and fell off his bed.

"A nightmare..."

He gasped, out of breath, before thinking a signal to turn on the lights and revealing his quarters at Jamestown. Other than him siting on the floor, everything was as it should be.

"Bizarre."

Raniero took a shower and tried to forget the worst parts of the dream. The communal bath was empty. Unusual, but Raniero hadn't looked at the clock, so maybe he just beat the morning rush.

The shower wasn't relaxing at all, really. The water was at best lukewarm, and all the closed space managed to do was dredge up imaginings of monsters lurking on the other side of the shower curtain.

He silently promised to go back and sign the water log later.

Afterwards, he went to the mess hall. The monitor

beside the kiosk called today's meal "cereal", but in reality it was little more than the usual pre-processed 3D printed dreck.

He didn't bother signing the food log, no one ever did.

He'd only started eating when a woman, a light brunette with a beauty mark beneath her left eye, sat across from him. Her ID tag read "Brin". He didn't know Dr. Melody Brin too well, beyond that she was the base psychiatrist and that she was attractive but by no means youthful. In fact, the more he thought about it, in the six months since he'd arrived on Mars he hadn't taken any time to get to know anyone. He knew their names, but considering everyone walked around with them emblazoned on their uniforms that wasn't much of an accomplishment. He supposed he must have spoken to Dr. Brin at least once before, but couldn't remember.

"So, how are you doing today? Any better?" she asked. Raniero swallowed some of the dismal cereal and shrugged.

"Fine, I suppose. Why?"

"Just checking," she replied. "You haven't exactly been in the best shape the last few months."

"Really?" Not sure how to take that, he simply shrugged. "Thank you, I guess, but I'm fine. Really." Melody nodded and smiled…not a friendly smile, but a comforting one. Raniero just stared. Without another word, Dr. Brin left the mess hall.

"Weird…"

Raniero's curiosity wouldn't to let Dr. Brin's words go. What was the point of that conversation? Also –

maybe he should have asked her, he now realized – why wouldn't that feeling of being watched go away? Raniero glanced over his shoulder at the next table, only for the conversation there to suddenly stop. Irritated atop his perplexity, he turned back to his meal. By the time he had swallowed another mouthful the other astronauts had rushed out.

While he dumped his bowl in the auto-sink, he wondered what dinner would be and glanced at the wall calendar. The spout stopped spitting recycled water long before he blinked again.

"That can't be right," he muttered. "It's March 31st, not June 16th…"

The dream came rushing back.

Raniero stumbled out of the mess hall and into Dr. Brin who, as it happened, was on her way back in. Much louder than he intended, Raniero shouted into her face:

"What day is it?!"

She stepped away from him.

"What?"

"What day is it?!" he shouted. "It's March 31st, right? Tell me it's the thirty-first!"

"Dr. Alba, are you feeling all right…?" she said.

Raniero grabbed her collar and shook.

"The day!" he shouted. "What's the damn day?!"

"Hey! What are you doing!"

"Stop it!"

"Grab him!"

Men descended on Raniero and pulled him off Brin. He screamed, almost hysterical:

"The day! Just tell me what day it is!"

One of the men grabbed Raniero in a headlock.

"Stop it! Calm down!" the astronaut—his nametag said Contador—said. "It's Sunday, remember? June 16th."

"No," Raniero said. "No, I don't remember!"

"Just calm down," Dr. Brin said. "Everything will be fine. Somebody call Commander Garcia!"

- - -

Raniero couldn't recall anything between the mess hall and sitting in Dr. Brin's office. He was calm now, although he wasn't sure why.

"I don't understand, Melody," he heard himself say, although he couldn't remember thinking those words. "I don't remember anything. Not even small flashes or glimpses...I only remember that day on Mare Platia, followed by waking up this morning. Was it really so long ago? I can't remember... and that scares me so much..."

She smiled.

"That's okay," Dr. Brin said. "Sometimes, amnesia can develop following such severe trauma..."

"What trauma?" Raniero said. "Everyone talks to me as if I know what's going on, as if I've been lucid for the last three months! What trauma? What happened? Please, fill me in here. I'm at a loss."

"I'm sorry," Dr. Brin said. "Three months ago, you were conducting a survey in the Mare Platia..."

"Yes, yes, I know that part already."

Patience when stressed was never a strength.

"What about the meteor?" Raniero said. "What happened in that crater?"

Dr. Brin's eyes narrowed and her head tilted.

"What meteor?" she said.

The two sat in silence for a full minute.

"Oh, I understand now," Dr. Brin said. "Your mind must have constructed its own memory of what happened, to make it easier for you to cope."

"What are you talking about?"

"Dr. Alba, there was no meteor." Dr. Brin said. She smiled and spoke soothingly in an effort to blunt reality.

"You and Dr. Mitamar were conducting a survey above a dried lava tube. The ground gave way."

Raniero stared, wordless.

"By the time the rescue team reached you, Dr. Mitamar was dead. You were unconscious due to oxygen deprivation and severe lacerations to the head..." She hesitated. "The clinic released you only a couple of days ago. They had been surprised you didn't suffer any permanent damage after everything you went through."

After a few moments, Raniero realized he should speak.

"Kemal is dead?"

Dr. Brin frowned.

"Yes," she said.

"And the meteor... it was all in my head?"

"Yes," she said. "It's a constructed memory, I think. I'm not sure about the cause of the amnesia, though...I can only recommend that you sign yourself back into the clinic for observation. It could be post-traumatic stress syndrome, or perhaps a result of the oxygen deprivation."

Raniero sighed, stood, and turned to the door.

"Thank you, Melody," he said. "Just...just give me a few minutes first."

"Of course."

He stepped out into the hallway.

"Raniero."

"Yes?" he said, and turned back to Dr. Brin.

"Hm?" she replied.

"Didn't you just call my name?"

She shook her head.

"Oh," Raniero said.

Without another word, he left.

He didn't go to the clinic. Instead, Raniero went straight back to his quarters, locked the door, turned the lights on, and went to bed, shivering.

This wasn't right.

He just knew, in his gut, that someone was lying. There was a meteor, he saw it and touched it...but what happened after that? What happened to him?

"Why can't I remember?"

"Raniero."

He hugged the blanket and buried his head under a pillow.

"Raniero."

He wasn't alone. It was watching him with those unfriendly eyes. It was in the room now, watching and taunting.

"Raniero."

"Leave me alone!"

"Sign your name, Raniero."

"Shut up! You're not real! You're in my head!"

"You'll never miss it. Look at all the pain it causes. Sign it to me, Raniero. Don't you want to be happy?"

"Shut! Up!"

Silence, but the presence didn't leave. It just kept watching.

Raniero preferred the voice.

An idea struck, and with feverish haste he scrambled for his desk. He tore open a drawer, dumping scrap paper and a copy of Dante before at last digging up a small white slab: his Flash Drive. He took a deep breath, and then plugged it into his room's computer terminal.

"Play the last recording," he commanded.

An affirmative beep, then:

"Testing, testing. I am Dr. Raniero Alba, here with Dr. Kemal Mitamar, from NASA Jamestown conducting Survey #9-19 at Mare Platia. It is March 30th, 2166…"

Raniero pressed the fast forward button on the computer's touch-screen monitor.

"…Believe it may be the meteorite, although I cannot yet explain the cause of the light emission. I'm going to take a closer look. O-okay… I have… apparently, stepped into some kind of air pocket…within the dust cloud. It's bright enough see without my lights, although there is no sunlight penetrating the dust. The light appears to be internally produced by…"

A pause. A grunt.

"Hello, Dr. Alba. I'm so pleased to meet you…" said the recording.

Behind him, the presence whispered:

"…Care to guess my name?"

Raniero couldn't scream, so he ran instead.

"Don't run, Raniero. Just sign your name. It'll all end if you just sign your name. That isn't hard, is it? You won't feel a thing and you won't lose a thing. No catch, no trick. Just sign your name. Do it, Raniero."

Somehow, the Voice had emptied Jamestown and distorted it into an endless, ever-changing maze. A dead shadow world saturated with pink dust.

A dream world.

"A dream…it's a dream!" Raniero shouted to no one. "It's not real! None of it is real!"

Suddenly the haze cleared, and Raniero was back in the crater standing before the Faberge egg and…himself. His doppelganger.

No, not quite – one eye was pupil-less.

The creature – dressed in a black double-breasted suit and an even blacker tie – stepped forward.

"Welcome back, doctor."

"I never left the crater, did I?" Raniero said. "All of that, everything at Jamestown, it was all a hallucination?"

It nodded its head.

"And you?"

"I caused the hallucination, but I am not the product of it," it said.

"Is Kemal dead?"

"No. He turned back." It grinned. "You did not."

Raniero gulped.

"Are you a Martian?"

It shook its head.

"But you are an ET, an alien. Right?"

It just grinned.

"Why?" Raniero said. "What do you want from me?"

"I want you."

"To do what?"

"I want to go home with you, to Indiana," It said. "That is all. No catch, no trick.

It unbuttoned its jacket and pulled out what appeared to be a small brown leather-bound notebook.

"Just sign your name and it'll be done."

"And why can't you just go yourself?" Raniero said.

"It is not so simple. There's a force around Earth that I cannot penetrate, not without the help of a man or woman. Help me, Raniero."

"Why?"

"Why?" It did not stop grinning. "If you don't help me, we'll just go through this again, and again. I'm patient."

"So I've done this before?" Raniero said.

"Oh, yes, many times now. Every time you've rejected my pleas, but I'm patient. Eventually, you will change your mind. It's inevitable. Each time the waveforms collapse differently, each iteration is just a little more different from the last. It is only a matter of time. I like you, Raniero. You're perfect, the best man on Mars to help me."

Raniero shut his eyes and sighed.

"Do it, Raniero."

It offered him a pen.

Raniero stepped forward and took it.

Queen of Fire Mountain

It had been many years since the villagers living at the bottom of Fire Mountain had made a sacrifice to their goddess.

Eudbia, the Queen of this mountain and realm, had once struck fear into the hearts of many, fighting ferocious battles with rivals in the skies above and raising the village every so often to remind the people of their place in her domain. But, during a particularly cold winter a few generations ago, she vanished. The arrogant of the time believed that the Monster had finally died, succumbing to her old age and the elements. The children of the arrogant came to believe that the Queen never even existed in the first place, shrugging off the stories of the elderly as just "myths and legends of a by-gone time".

In truth, Eudbia was neither old nor dead.

In fact, by the standards of her race she was still quite young and vibrant. A few centuries were nothing to her, neither was a three-quarter century slumber. If the arrogant and their descendants were so sure of her death or non-existence, they surely would have taken the trek to Eudbia's lair near the summit of Fire Mountain to look for themselves, but they were so blinded by their arrogance they never once chose to do it. Thus, for nearly seventy-five years the Queen of Fire Mountain rested at the top of her mountain, unaware of the great human insurgency that washed over her realm.

Eudbia awoke on an unusually warm spring afternoon, and almost immediately she sensed that things were not as they should be. The air smelled different. As she stretched the kinks out of her legs, Eudbia walked out the entrance of her lair into the bright blue day. She purred as the sunlight warmed her skin, her tail, her wings and her snout. At the bottom of the mountain now rested a large city, teeming with thousands of the tiny vermin. Those insolent wretches! They dared to claim her land as their own? This insult would not go unpunished.

With a mighty roar, Eudbia opened her wings and descended upon the town. In her first pass, she just skimmed over the rooftops to get a closer look at what the humans had done in the time since she last stirred, letting her backdraft tear the roofs off of the houses and shops. In her second pass she let loose her fury, breathing plumes of smoke and flame into the streets. She snorted as the smell of singed flesh and hair reached her nostrils. After several more passes, Eudbia returned to her lair, leaving the town a burning ruin.

Now Eudbia left it to the villagers to decide what their fate would be. Their forefathers had always been wise: sacrificing a young virgin in a meager attempt to placate their master. While not particularly satisfying, Eudbia had always believed that the message was still loud and clear: "Forgive us, liege. You are the rightful Queen of this realm, God save your soul!" This generation, though, was ruled by the arrogant. They were quick to pass off the Queen's punishment as the wild rampage of a dumb beast, a beast that must be eliminated for the sake of their so-called nation. Eudbia watched, disgusted, as an army was amassed against her. The humans want war? Those foolish vermin, what do they hope to prove with their slaughter?

Eudbia let the first contingent climb as high as her lair. They were so sure of themselves, armed with their wooden sticks and metal pokers. Their leader, sitting atop a magnificent white horse, raised a saber and gave the order to charge. Eudbia couldn't help but smile at the audacity, before opening her maw and burning them all to death. It wasn't long before the villagers tried again, although this time they tried a somewhat more interesting method: hurling burning boulders using wooden contraptions. If anything, these arrogant vermin were ingenious craftsmen. Eudbia took to the air, swooped down upon the catapults, and incinerated them with ease.

It took only moments for the humans to regroup and attack again, this time sending a cloud of arrows into the sky after the Queen. Several flew only a breadth away from

Eudbia's flesh, but a flap of the wings and she was clear of the first volley. In order to avoid the second she makes a broad turn and flew straight for the heart of town. This, however, was her first mistake. The villagers had anticipated a second attack on the town and installed a series of fortifications, a dozen of which immediately opened fire. None of the ballista bolts managed to hit Eudbia, but a few of the arrows did. She screeched loudly as they bit into her flesh, but none drew blood from her armored skin.

The Queen decided to swoop down into the town itself, using the tall spires near the center of town as protection from the ballistas. It was not long before a third contingent of villagers, all these dressed from head to toe in shiny metal armor of their own, discovered her. These humans, though, seemed to be true warriors worthy of facing their master in combat. They split into three groups, the main two attempting to surround Eudbia and trap her in the narrow streets. She roared and charged both groups at once, slashing with her claws and thrashing with her tail. But, while the armored warriors were easy to knock over and toss around, they proved far more difficult to actually kill. Several plunged their swords into Eudbia, piercing her armored skin and finally staining her olive hide. Angry, she breathed fire on them and reveled in their agonized screams for a moment before another warrior stabbed her in the side. She grabbed him in her jaws and crushed the life out of him. But, as she tossed the corpse aside, she spotted the third group of warriors trying to sneak up from behind. The bastards! They pulled off a flank!

With not enough room to spread out her wings here, Eudbia dug her claws into one of the towers and began to climb. Very quickly the air filled with arrows, many striking her back, tail, and wings. She climbed higher, faster, trying to get as high as possible. If she could get high enough, the arrows could not reach her and she could get back into the air. Finally, Eudbia reached the top of the tower, spread open her wings...and reeled as an errant ballista bolt slammed into her breast. For a moment, her mind was blank, and there was no sound but the wind blowing past her ears. She was dizzy and disillusioned. Somehow, she managed to grab hold of the tower's peak before she could fall and collect herself.

Eudbia looked down at the wound, and at once knew that it was fatal. With a grunt, the Queen took hold of the bolt and ripped it out of her chest, tossing the bloody rod down to the streets. Her blood now flowed in rivers, staining her belly, her claws, and the tower. She could even taste it in her mouth now. Eudbia coughed as a trickle dripped from her mouth. It would not be long now. She clutched the wound and decided to take in one last view of her realm. Even as she felt her wounded heart slow, she found herself smiling: she had managed to climb the tallest of the human towers. How fitting. Eudbia let loose one more majestic roar, closed her eyes, and let go of the tower's peak.

By the time she fell to the Earth, the Queen was gone.

Immediately, the villagers began to celebrate their victory, boasting of their slaying the "Beast of Fire Mountain". Word soon spread throughout the human world, tales of valiant knights battling the bloodthirsty monster in the streets, of its fateful ascent and grizzly death. From the humans the word spread to the more compassionate of the Queen's race, and from them to the less compassionate, until it at last reached the one named Jagetab. Long before Queen Eudbia had fallen into her decades-long slumber, she had been with another, and from him bore her only offspring, the heir to her realm.

Ten years after the death of Eudbia, after the fateful spring day when the vermin rose up to overthrow their master, death returned. It came in the night, breathing fire and wreaking unbridled destruction. By morning, the human town was nothing but a smoldering memory.

For Jagetab, the King of Fire Mountain, there was nothing sweeter than vengeance.

Castle at the Icicle's Edge

24 June 1906

My Dearest Lucinda,

I do not know if this letter will ever reach you from the dark and cold expanse of wasteland I have found myself trapped in, but I can only pray that it does. I hope the world eventually learns what has happened to our expedition and what we have discovered in the Arctic Circle.

We found a castle, built on the shore of the Arctic Sea. It seemed abandoned at the time, understandable considering its age. But, that was the very thing that confused us: it appeared to be Medieval in origin! I could swear it was Gothic in origin, but I have never heard of Germans ever establishing a colony in Canada, and certainly not during the era of castle building. How could this place exist?

We investigated further, and explored the ruins.

This place really does seem to be as old as it appears. Everything is covered in a foot of dust and ice, anything made of wood is rotted to nearly the point of total disintegration. We found a library, or what remained of one, but could not find anything salvageable that could give us a clue. It is a large estate, clearly intended to house at least fifty servants along with the owner, yet we could find no evidence of what became of it's residents. Some rooms were untouched, yet others showed signs of some sort of struggle.

We wrote it all off as odd and decided to make camp inside.

My God, we made a horrible mistake.

There is a horror here, Lucinda. A horror that we could never have anticipated.

A monster. A beast.

It looks like a man, so much like a man, but it is not. It is relentless, it is bloodthirsty, and it has only impossibly deep darkness where eyes should be. It moves about the dark as if it were daylight, as calmly as you or I would during a nice stroll in the park, but always in pursuit of its next victim.

I think a man created this thing. The very same who built this place, perhaps. We found a room filled with evidence of satanic ritual and someone having practiced the dark arts, but it has been long abandoned like the rest of this infernal ruin.

Whoever summoned this thing, he is dead now. But, his monster, it lives and continues to stalk us night and day. It has already killed Walter and Abraham. Jeremiah is hurt badly. I don't think he will survive the next night. And I...I don't know how long my sanity will stay intact.

I hear footsteps. Farewell, Lucinda.

Sincerely,
Powell

- - -

10 October 1913

After years of searching, I think I have finally found where my beloved Powell disappeared.

Our expedition has found a castle on the Arctic coast, a relic none of our party can explain. It is old and worn, perhaps even Medieval in origin. I know that cannot be so. I find it disturbing that it appears on none of our charts, even though there have been men through this area before. How could no one have known about this place? It is enormous!

But still...is this what you found, my love? What happened here that made you not return to me? Are you alive at all?

There is an ominous gloom in the air around this place. There are no birds. The silence is very unnerving.

Armand, our guide, has suggested we turn back and return with a larger party, but I have rejected that plan. I have not spent so much of my inheritance and devoted this much time, only to turn back now! I must find Powell. I will not turn back now that I am so close, so very close. I swear I can hear him calling to me, his voice is faint but I know in my heart it is there.

We will set up camp tonight outside the castle. Tomorrow, Ishmael, Dawson, and I will make a preliminary investigation of the interior.

October 12, 1913

Ishmael is dead.

I have been a fool. I should never have come to this horrid place. The monster isn't far now, I can hear it howling somewhere on the other side of the door. I've locked myself in. There is a window I can escape through, but I don't think I can run fast enough to escape the creature.

I found Powell's letter. He is dead too, dead for at least eight years. What was I thinking? I should have listened to Armand two days ago and turned back. Even if we had returned with a larger party.

No.

I doubt they would have had any greater success. The monster is immortal.

I think it has found me.

- - -

TOP SECRET
FOR YOUR EYES ONLY

19 July 1915

To the Prime Minister:

On the evening of 11 November 1913, a man calling himself Armand appeared at   Royal Northwest Mounted Police outpost at [REDACTED]. He was terribly wounded and in shock. He identified himself as a member of a rescue expedition launched from Ottawa on 25 July and claimed that his party had found an enormous ruin about fifty kilometers north-northwest from the outpost. He also claimed that a ferocious creature of some kind had murdered nearly all of his party.

The man described a creature that looked much like a man but with skin faded to a sickly gray pallor, horrible surgical or industrial scars, and empty eye sockets. Yet, despite its appearance this individual was inhumanly strong, as fast as a horse at full gallop, and by his description had incredible senses of smell and hearing—so much so that Armand believed he or it could see despite the lack of eyes.

We were unable to glean anything further, as the man's mind appeared to have broken. The officers sent him away and, since, he has been interned at the Insane

Asylum at [REDACTED].

After some discussion, it was decided that a party would be dispatched to investigate the incident. Five officers, [REDACTED], left the outpost on 13 November, armed and well-provisioned.

On the evening of 1 December, one returned. His story was remarkably similar to Armand's tale, reporting that the officers had located the ruin and an abandoned camp but, at first, no one else. No corpses nor any other sign of habitation. They camped outside the ruin with plans to investigate further the next day, but were ambushed in the night by an individual matching the previous witness' description. In the ensuing encounter, all but Officer [REDACTED] were killed by means of strangulation and blunt force by the assailant. By his account, the individual or creature appeared impervious to gunfire or blades.

The officer died shortly afterwards.

Report of the incident was relayed back to headquarters in Ottawa. After a private meeting was held between [REDACTED] to discuss the matter, it was recommended that the matter be handed to the Department of Militia and Defense. This was done formally, though quietly, on 30 December 1913.

At the command of [REDACTED], a Permanent Force battalion of three hundred and ten men was ordered to advance in secret, locate the individual in question, and to secure the area.

The Permanent Force battalion arrived on the afternoon of 14 June 1914, and quickly confirmed the existence of the ruins. Film and photographic evidence of this has been attached to the report. Lieutenant Colonel Audrey Thompson, the commanding officer, ordered thirty men to enter the ruins and search for the missing officers and civilians. Within a half hour, gunfire was heard from inside the ruin but, unsure of the situation inside, Lt. Col. Thompson did not send in more men. After an additional ten minutes, twenty of the original thirty militiamen emerged from the ruin, most wounded, and being pursued by what Lt. Col. Thompson could only describe as a "MONSTER".

Lt. Col. Thompson ordered the battalion to open fire.

Regular small arms fire appeared ineffective and the creature—Thompson insists that the individual be referred to as such—killed another three of his men during this exchange.

Rifle and pistol fire ineffective, Thompson ordered his men to fall back while automatic weapons—a pair of 7.7 millimeter Vickers machine guns—were set up and deployed. These appeared to slow it down and, eventually, it grew tired of the combat and returned to the ruins.

Over the course of this first engagement, lasting no more than one hundred and fifty minutes, thirteen men were killed. Their killer, whoever or whatever it was, by Lt. Col. Thompson's account, was no worse for wear.

It was at this point that Lt. Col. Thompson determined the only real avenue left would be bombardment. After setting camp at what was considered a minimum safe distance, a messenger was dispatched requesting artillery.

Two cannons, pulled by motorcar, were dispatched

from [REDACTED] and reached Thompson's battalion on the morning of 15 July. Wasting no time, Lt. Col. Thompson ordered the artillery into position. Bombardment began by 1200 hours that same day.

The creature reemerged from the ruins within an hour, agitated by the attack. Lt. Col. Thompson promptly ordered the artillery to focus its bombardment on the creature. After a combination of machine gun fire and artillery bombardment during which it was struck by three shells directly, it at last was killed.

After making sure it was dead, Lt. Col. Thompson ordered the remains blown up with six tons of TNT.

The bodies of at least fifty men and women were recovered from the ruins afterwards. The oldest remains, believed to be [REDACTED], date to at least 1885.

It is the opinion of this officer that the Royal Canadian Navy shell the ruins and all trace of this incident expunged from all official records.

Sincerely,

Major-General Sir W.G. Gwatkin
Chief of the General Staff

- - -

9 July 2023

Have I got a story for you! As you guys already know, my job at the Canadian national archives is pretty damn boring.   Half the time, I just snoop through old government files and stuff.

It's fun reading TOP SECRET stuff!

But, what I found today was weird.

It was a bunch of letters and stuff from back at the start of the twentieth.

I have no idea what was going on, but it sounds like some kind of military operation in the far north. Something about a monster and a castle...

Catalonia

Two lonely figures stroll down the dark and dusty dirt road in the pale moonlight. One, a tall young man, walks slowly. Hunched slightly, his hands are stuffed into his coat pockets while his eyes seem glued to the ground before him. A sigh escapes his lips, revealing his deep disappointment with himself.

The young man's companion, a slightly shorter and older man, conveys a far different mood. He stands tall and walks briskly, one hand carrying an oil lamp while the other is balled into a tight fist. His eyes are cold and his face indifferent.

"Quit your sulking, Patrick," he growls, "It had to be done and you know it." Patrick doesn't respond for a long time, but when he does his voice can barely be heard:

"I'm dirt." Obviously angry, the shorter man leaps into his companion's path.

"I said stop crying!" he yells, "Stop crying for that damned slacker!"

"He's my friend, Rodger," Patrick quietly shouts back, "and I've let him down. I should never have asked you to come with me."

"Friends…" replies Rodger sarcastically, "There's no need for friends…especially crippled men who won't even try to work!"

"Rodger, please…"

Rodger looks the man up and down before turning away, disgusted.

"In the morning, I'm sending my men to take possession of Mr. Trilby's house. The bank will be receiving its money, Patrick, and there is nothing you can say or do to stop us," he says, "Even though we're cousins, it does not mean your so-called friends get a free pass on their debts, no matter what the circumstances may be."

Content with this, Rodger is about to continue on his way when, suddenly, he hears something. A voice…no louder than a whisper, but it is definitely a voice.

"Did you hear that?" asks Patrick. Rodger turns to face his cousin, but immediately spots the source of the mysterious sound. In the distance, not too far down the road behind them, stands the silhouette of a woman. Her curvy figure, illuminated by the moonlight, seems like a ghostly apparition…a figure plucked from the pages of some terrifying tome. Again the whisper comes, and both men strain to make out the words.

"Help," she seems to quietly say, "Help..." Immediately, Rodger finds himself in the grip of a deep fear. He remembers the stories, those silly stories he and his friends told each other in the darkest of nights, those stories of witches, demons, and ghosts. His own silent fears and superstitions, things which he had believed he'd long vanquished, suddenly welled up inside him, consuming his rational mind completely. Terrified, he starts to turn away. Suddenly, Patrick grabs his arm.

"What are you doing?" he asks, "She needs our help!" Eyes wide with terror, panic, and fear, Rodger pushes his cousin away.

"Let go of me you idiot!" he growls just before scampering away into the darkness. Now alone in the gloom, Patrick turns towards the shadowy woman. Swallowing his fear, the young man goes to her. As he approaches, the shadows shrink away, revealing a seductive beauty. Her flowing blonde hair waves silently in the chilled autumn breeze, her luscious curves glow in the pale light, and Patrick finds himself frozen, awestruck, at the sight of this angelic figure.

"Is...is everything okay?" Pat finally stammers, "I...I thought...I heard you call for help." The beauty's silken white robes flutter as another breeze blows past. She shivers.

"Yes," she replies in a very thick Germanic accent, "I'm lost."

"Ah, I understand," says Patrick, a bit more relaxed as he smiles caringly. He unbuttons his coat and offers it to her. "Please, take it. I will lead you back to town."

"Thank you," the beauty replies as she pulls it on, "Thank you." Patrick gently takes the woman's soft, tender hand and leads her towards the light of civilization. For a while, there is only silence, nothing but the occasional leaf crushing underfoot and the rare hoot of an owl. Finally, Patrick musters the courage to break the silence.

"Um…my name is Pat," he says.

"I am Catalonia," the beauty replies. Pat smiles.

"Catalonia…that's a very beautiful name."

"Do you think so?" the beauty says, "It was my mother's name."

Patrick turns to Catalonia and asks, "How is it that you ended up lost this deep in the forest, this late at night, all by yourself?"

"Well, I was taking my afternoon stroll with my husband, when Alan, that wretched old fool, suddenly appeared. We argued briefly and soon we went on our way. After the stars started to become clear in the sky, my husband and I decided to make our way back home. Suddenly, a big black…"

Catalonia's voice trails away when she notices Pat's smile fade a bit, before turning and looking ahead. She frowns slightly. Did she say something wrong?

"Are you okay? Is something bothering you?" asks Catalonia.

"No…no, I just have many things on my mind," Pat replies quietly. He soon slows to a stop.

"Pat?"

"I…I'm such a coward," he mutters, "A coward and a traitor."

"What...?"

Patrick's gaze drifts to his feet as he explains, "My friend, Corbin Trilby, hurt his back in an accident at work not too long ago. The pain is so bad that he cannot work anymore. My cousin, Rodger, works for the bank. He says that Corbin must still pay off his loans, despite the injury, or he'll go to jail. I...I thought if I could just explain to him the pain Corbin is in...how he simply isn't fit to work..."

Crunch, crunch, crunch. Catalonia looks back, and her face pales in fear.

"I...I'm worthless as a friend. How could I bring Rodger to see Corbin? I was a fool to believe that would convince him. All I did was betray a good friend..."

"Pa...Pat..."

Patrick snaps out of his angsty stupor and looks up at the terror-stricken Catalonia. It's then that he sees it: a dark beast, blacker than the shadows and with eyes the color of blood. A wolf.

"Get behind me," the young man whispers, slowly moving in between the beauty and the horrid beast. Suddenly, the wolf leaps, throwing Patrick to the ground. It lunges at Pat's jugular, but the man is able to wrap his hands around the wolf's neck, mustering all of his strength to simultaneously hold it back and strangle it. Catalonia backs away fearfully as the two struggle to kill each other. Pat knees its gut. The wolf claws Pat's chest. The beast's jaws inch closer and closer to the man's flesh, its dagger-like fangs glistening a terrible ivory white.

Without warning, there is a sudden flash of light, a

shattering of glass, and a spray of crimson. Pat watches the wolf's eyes dilate and he feels all of its muscles stiffen. A thud and the wolf flops to the side, dead. Confused, Pat looks up and finds himself surprised at the identity of his savior.

"R…Rodger?" he pants, "What are…where…how…?" Rodger sighs and helps his cousin to his feet.

"I…I'm sorry, Pat," he says. Now Patrick is very confused. Rodger? Apologizing?!

"You see," Rodger explains, "I made it about halfway back to town before I stopped and thought, 'What am I doing? I am Rodger Stillman, and Rodger Stillman flees from nothing.' So…I turned around and came back for you." Rodger sighs again.

"Rodger…are you…?"

"I felt guilty, okay?!" Rodger suddenly snaps, "I shouldn't have yelled at you, I shouldn't have run away, and I shouldn't have left you behind! I'm sorry." Rodger then turns his attention to the all but forgotten Catalonia.

"Come on now," she says, offering his hand to help her up, "Let's get out of here before the rest of that bastard's pack shows up."

Finally, about half an hour later, Patrick, Rodger, and Catalonia emerge from the woods into the rustic town of Midsford. Rodger sighs, relieved that that experience had ended. Well…almost.

"Patrick," he finally says, "I've come to a decision."

"Oh?"

"I've decided…" Rodger pauses, unsure of what to say next. Is this really what he wants to say? He finds it hard

to believe that he has even considered it. Then again...
"I've...changed my mind."

Pat freezes in mid-step.

"What...?" he barely breathes. Rodger stops as well, but does not turn to face his cousin.

"I've decided not to send my men tomorrow. I will give your friend more time."

Pat is, quite literally, shocked. From the moment Rodger reappeared and killed the wolf, it seems as if his personality has made a complete 180 degree turn. What happened to him?

"Wh...Why?" Pat asks incredulously.

"I..." Rodger pauses again, but quickly continues, "After I left you in the woods, I was intent on disowning you and throwing Mr. Trilby in jail for tax evasion. I had no intention of ever going back for you. But...then... something struck me. It was like a dull pain, deep in my gut...for some reason, it made me think of you, of Mr. Trilby, and of the lady. I don't know why...but...I had this feeling...and it told me to go back. That I was wrong, you were in danger, and I had to go back. So, I went back."

Rodger turns to Patrick, and smiles. For a few moments, Pat just stands there and stares, dumbfounded, at his cousin. Finally, he leaps forward and wraps his arms around Rodger in a tight embrace.

"Thank you," he whispers, "Thank you, Rodger. Thank you." The beauty turns to her escorts and smiles brightly, glad to see everything end happily.

"I want to thank you both," she says, "I was afraid we would never make it." Catalonia steps closer and kisses both men on the cheek. "You're angels!"

"Oh…it was…um…no problem," Patrick replies, his face blushing. Catalonia starts to take off Pat's coat, intending to return it to him, but he quickly stops her.

"Don't worry, just take it," he says, "I have another at home." Catalonia smiles.

"Thank you," she says gratefully, "I should go now. Goodbye!"

"Yes, you have a good night now, Miss," says Rodger. After one last wave, Catalonia walks away.

As the two men watch her depart, Patrick turns to Rodger and asks, "Rodger, why did you run away when you saw Catalonia before?"

"It was stupid," he replies, smiling to himself, "Remember that story grandfather used to tell us when we were little?"

"Do you mean the one about the murdered woman who haunted the woods?" Pat laughs, "You were afraid because of an old ghost story?"

"Yeah…I told you it was stupid."

The two men watch Catalonia for a few more moments and are about to go home themselves when the most astonishing thing happens: like a wisp of smoke, the beautiful Catalonia vanishes into thin air!

Man of the Century

"Has it said anything?" asks Auzhan.

The creature on the other side of the glass looks far different from the robust beast it appeared to be in the original photo's he'd been given, now that the interrogators have had a few hours with it. Stripped, beaten, and dried blood covering half of its bruised face have done much to wipe the callous smirk it originally had.

"Nothing useful. At least, nothing I could understand," replies Pouriya, the Deputy Chief of Police for Kerman, "The ones before you have included everything relevant in the file." Auzhan leafs through the flimsy scribbled pages again:

"Kttal Miller. Chief Master Sergeant. Serial Number: 980012436. Speaks little to no Farsi, but is fluent in

English," Auzhan reads. "This isn't much to go on."

"No. He's stubborn," replies Pouriya, "Besides that, I assume you know the other relevant information about the crash?"

"I was at the site before driving here," says Auzhan, "I couldn't make any more sense of it than anyone else."

"If the Americans really do have the capability to build spacecraft like that, our country may be in serious danger," replies the Deputy Chief, "This could change the world's balance of power."

"The President and the Supreme Leader want a preliminary report in two hours," Auzhan says, handing the folder back to Pouriya, "Make sure the security camera is recording everything. I think it's time I get acquainted with our little green friend."

In truth, the creature chained up in the interrogation room is neither little nor green. Shorter than the average man, yes, but not by much. Auzhan likened him to a dragon or dinosaur, a reptilian thing from the depths of hellish space. It stirred little when Auzhan opened the door, and raised its eyes for only a moment as Auzhan stepped in front of it. The creature, despite looking like a man-snake, looked to have skin of the same texture and fragility of any normal human. Rather than the green one might expect, its skin looked dark, like the color of wet earth.

"Kttal Miller. Chief Master Sergeant. 980012436," it says quietly in impeccable English.

"A pleasure to meet you, Sergeant Miller. I am Auzhan Sabouri."

The creature's head suddenly snaps up, its eyes wide with surprise. Then, just as suddenly, it bursts out laughing! Auzhan takes a step away, confused.

"Sabouri?" the creature laughs, "Auzhan Sabouri? Oh, this is just TOO MUCH!"

"What's so funny?" growls Auzhan, not appreciating being the butt of a joke nobody has told him.

"God, I thought this was the sort of thing that only happened in bad action movies," it says, not exactly answering Auzhan's question. His confusion turning to anger, Auzhan backhands the creature's face although it does little to stop the laughing. He grabs the creature's snout and forces it to face him.

"What is so funny?" Auzhan hisses.

"That the President of Iran has come to interrogate me personally," the creature replies. Auzhan is taken aback.

"I'm not the President..." says Auzhan. The creature's grin begins to fade.

"Of course you are. It's January 2017. You've been in office for six months," the creature says. Auzhan shakes his head.

"No," he says, "Today is January 11, 2007." The creature stares at Auzhan, stunned silent. It's gaze slowly turns away from Auzhan and becomes fixed at a crack in the cement floor.

"Son of a bitch..." it whispers, "I'm dead."

"You don't have to be," Auzhan replies, "If you just answer my questions..."

"I can't."

"Yes, you can. You will," says Auzhan.

"No, I can't!" shouts the creature, "I don't know anything!"

"Everyone knows something," replies Auzhan, "Considering the aircraft you were aboard, I'd say you know quite a bit more than something."

"No, you don't get it!" the creature shouts again, "I can't tell you anything useful! I... I'm not even BORN yet!"

"What...?"

"My name... is Kttal Miller," it whispers, "I was born on August 3, 2379, in Portland, Oregon."

"That's... that's bullshit!" shouts Auzhan, "That's impossible!"

"I joined the Air Force in 2398. I was stationed aboard the Jefferson Avery four years after that," it explains, "We were on our way back to Earth when our engines malfunctioned. We lost control. I don't remember much between that and when your friends chained me up here."

Auzhan eyes the video camera in the corner of the room before asking: "Why are you telling me this? You haven't said much more than your name until now. Why...?"

"Isn't it obvious? You're Auzhan Sabouri," it replies.

"I don't know what that means!" shouts Auzhan, "How do you know me?"

"Everyone knows you," says the creature, "You're the most important person of this century..." Again, Auzhan looks to the security camera, the little red light blinking menacingly. Suddenly, he leaps at the creature and batters it, again and again, until his hand grows numb and the creature's face is covered with fresh blood. Then, he grabs the creature in a headlock and begins to squeeze. The creature struggles to breathe, its contortions violent enough to nearly knock both Auzhan and itself down.

"I serve at the pleasure of the Supreme Leader and the President!" Auzhan hisses, "Your lies will not confuse me into betraying them!" The creature gasps, trying to respond but without enough breath to do so. "Who built that ship? Where do you come from? How long have the Americans had contact?"

"I... don't..."

"Tell me, or I'll snap your neck!"

"Do it."

Auzhan looks straight into the creature's eyes. He loosens his grip somewhat, but doesn't let go.

"You're willing to die for the Americans?" he asks.

"Don't you get it? I am American," the creature replies, "But, no one is going to come for me. Nobody knows I exist. First Contact isn't for at least another 30 years."

"You don't have to die," says Auzhan, "Help us. We will return you to your country and you can explain all of this to them."

"What for?" it asks, "My family, my world doesn't exist yet. First Contact isn't for at least another 30 years. I'll be alone. And..." It shuts its eyes. "History must proceed according to plan. I'm going to die anyway. I have to die."

"History isn't written," replies Auzhan.

"It is," the creature states, "Time is a fixed line. What has happened has, it cannot be changed. I have to die and you have to survive, to be President. That's what must happen."

"Survive?" asks Auzhan, but the creature doesn't reply. "What are you talking about? What does 'survive' mean?!"

"It was an honor to meet you... Mr. Sabouri."

Auzhan squeezes the creature's neck again. It struggles, eyes wide, jaws snapping. After a few moments, its motions grow slow and sluggish. At last, it falls limp. He lets go. He looks towards the security camera once again. Then, he walks out.

"Did you kill it?" asks Pouriya.

"No, it's just unconscious," Auzhan replies, "Did you catch anything of what we said?"

"No, not even the gist. I don't understand enough English," says the Deputy Chief. Auzhan nods.

"That's fine. I have enough information to make my report. Where is the tape?" Pouriya hands him a little black square of plastic -- a run-of-the-mill DV tape. Auzhan drops it and smashes it to pieces beneath his heel.

"What are you doing?!" shouts Pouriya.

"Surviving."

With a sudden snap of the wrist, Auzhan knocks the Deputy Chief unconscious. He watches as the fat little man crumples, as disbelieving as Pouriya. He shoves the doubt out of his mind – there's no time to consider that. He tears the keys from Pouriya's belt and then rushes to unchain... Miller. His name is Miller.

Kttal gasps as Auzhan pulls him from the chair, every muscle and bone in his body probably screaming in pain from the blows he's been dealt.

"Keep quiet," hisses Auzhan, "There's no time. Stay

quiet."

Auzhan drags Miller past Pouriya, who has just started to stir again. Ignoring him, Auzhan leans against the wall, reaches over, and raps on the door.

"Hey! We need some help in here!" he shouts. The door unlatches and swings open slowly. The first guard, seeing the bleeding form of the Deputy Chief on the floor, rushes to help the man. The second guard does the same, but doesn't make it more than a step into the room before his face meets the butt of Auzhan's handgun. The other guard immediately turns, his hand reaching for his own service pistol, but Auzhan is faster to aim.

"Don't even think about it," he growls, "Unbuckle your holster and throw it in the corner over there. Then go in the interrogation room and shut the door." Slowly, the man does as he's told. As soon as the other door shuts, Auzhan and Miller stumble out into the hall. Again Miller groans, this time as if he were trying to say something but just failing to form words.

"Not yet. Just hold on," Auzhan whispers.

Auzhan and Miller stumble through the hallway both covered in Miller's blood, stumbling, hissing, and grunting. The hallway is dark and long. There's a single light and it glows dimly. There's an elevator at the end, Auzhan immediately rushes for it. He stumbles against the wall, but keeps pushing forward, dragging Miller along, and forcing him further. He pass a door just as a police officer walks out. Auzhan points his gun at him.

"Back off! Back off!"

The police officer is more shocked by the naked

bleeding creature hanging off of Auzhan's shoulder than the gun itself and does exactly what the interrogator asks. Finally, they reach the elevator. Auzhan punches the down button with the butt of his gun just as several more officers, their guns drawn, pour into the hallway. Their eyes are wide, shocked, confused, not sure what the hell they're looking at or what the hell is actually happening but sure that whatever it is, this man is in front of them, whatever this creature is, must not leave the police station.

"Calm down! Calm down! Relax!" one of the officers says, slowly lowering his weapon, "We can talk about this. Let's just stay calm. What's happening? Who are you? Who... what is this thing?"

Auzhan doesn't bother responding. The elevator doors open behind him, they slide inside and he hits the close button. The elevator plummets to the parking garage beneath the police station. Auzhan catches his breath and glances at Miller, just to be sure that he's there, that he's alive... that he exists. Again, Miller attempts to speak uttering something between a 'thank you' and a 'why'. But again, Auzhan just whispers:

"Be quiet. Not yet."

The elevator doors open and Auzhan bursts out, not quite running but moving as fast as he can away from the door towards the far end of the parking garage where he left his car. He just makes it past the first line of cars by the time the officers from upstairs finally appear from the stairwell. They rush towards him, their guns drawn but not aiming – too confused, too unsure of what's really happening to take the chance of shooting this man.

Auzhan can't take that chance, though, and opens fire. He shoots once, twice, shattering the driver's side window of a pick-up truck and putting bullet holes in the windshield of a police cruiser. One of the officers fire back, his bullet hitting the pavement and bouncing into the car beside Auzhan and Miller. Auzhan dives, nearly throwing Miller to the ground. He leaps over the prone creature, reaches around the side of the car and fires several more times at the officers.

Ducking behind the car again, Auzhan wraps Miller's arm around his shoulder more firmly and whispers to Miller:

"All right. I need your help. I'm not strong enough to run and carry you at the same time. I need you to run. Can you do that?" Miller nods. "Good. Now!"

The two run from their hiding place. Not very fast – Miller is pretty much limping, but Auzhan pulls him along. They slam into the hood of Auzhan's car, barely ducking before several more bullets make some holes in Auzhan's windshield. Auzhan pushes Miller into the gap between the cars, pulls the driver side door open, and shoves him inside before crawling in after. He fumbles with the keys, first unable to find the right key, and then get that damn key into the damn keyhole, but finally the key turns and the car roars to life and off they go. Tires screeching, Auzhan careens through the cramped parking garage, his head almost below the dashboard. A police officer jumps in front of the car and fires, but seeing that the driver isn't where he should be dives out the way again only a moment before he would be killed. Auzhan makes a sharp turn, plows through the security gate, and emerges onto a busy downtown street. Auzhan's car, scratched and shot up, swerves through traffic and avoids several cars that honk angrily as he speeds by.

Not willing to give his pursuers any opportunity to catch up, he makes a sudden turn down a back alley and then a down another, out onto a side street. His path is a zigzag, almost completely random, taking him to a part of the city he's not familiar with. Despite this, he knows exactly what he's doing, where he's going, and where he wants to be. That place is simple: anywhere except in this city... he needs to get Miller out of Kerman.

Miller, now crumpled into a small bleeding ball, finally begins to stir. He rolls slightly, having enough presence of mind to know he mustn't be seen by anyone outside, tilts his head up and looks at Auzhan. He doesn't try to speak, he just simply looks. Auzhan can feel his eyes drilling into the side of his face, but doesn't turn to look, he just ignores it. There's no time. This isn't the place to ask questions or demand answers.

It must be hours later by the time they finally escape the city and make it out into the countryside. Auzhan turns off the main road and onto a lonely dirt path. He knows this road, he's been here before... no one who works at the pleasure of the Supreme Leader or the President can avoid knowing about those particular back roads, the ones where the enemies of the Revolution are made to vanish forever. At last, with the sun hanging low in the sky, Auzhan pulls over. He sits in silence for a long while, before glancing toward Miller. Miller glances back.

Auzhan gets out of the car. Miller shakily, partly from the beatings and partly from laying the same uncomfortable position for so long, sits up.

Auzhan lights a cigarette and starts walking toward what appears to be a concrete storage shed half concealed in the dried brush. He swipes his ID card and enters the key code – thank goodness for non-integrated electronics. He doesn't need to be here long regardless.

Miller's head is still throbbing and he's got at least a broken rib. The passenger's side door opens.

"Put this on," said Auzhan, dropping a shirt and pants on his lap.

"Why?" Miller whispers hoarsely, "Why are you doing this?" He doesn't look at Auzhan or reach for the clothes. Auzhan sucks a drag.

"I love my country. I'll do whatever it takes to defend it," he replies, breathing a smoke cloud. Miller eyes the interrogator expressionlessly.

"But... you're betraying it..." he mutters.

"There's more than one way to express love," Auzhan replies. He steps away and turns toward the distant foothills. "Get dressed so we can get out of here."

"And go where?" asks Miller as he slips on the egregiously large shirt. To himself, he also wonders what the point would be. The world as he knows it won't exist for centuries, and unless everything he learned about time travel in high school physics was wrong... there's no going home, and no changing the past. He's as good as dead anyway.

"South," said Auzhan, "To Bandar-e 'Abbas. I know

some people there who we can trust, who can get you across the Gulf to the UAE."

With considerable effort, Miller pulls himself to his feet. Leaning against the car, he tries pulling on the pants. Of course, they are designed for humans rather than his own species... and are two sizes too small. Miller grumbles a few curses that Auzhan doesn't recognize... he'd say not English, but there's no telling what ways the language will change by the 24th century. It's really more remarkable that Auzhan can understand Miller at all.

"Enjoying your vacation to the dark ages so far?"

Miller laughs cynically. "Loving every minute. Your people are so hospitable."

"We aim to please," Auzhan replies, tossing the spent cigarette.

It was night when Auzhan and Miller pulled up in front of a run-down tenement by the docks, the only light coming from a nearly burnt out streetlight. After sending a text message, Auzhan tossed Miller a headscarf.

"Extra security."

A window opened on the third floor – the safety signal. Auzhan and Miller rushed from the car to an open door. Miller eyed the man holding it open for them, but Auzhan whispered assurances that he was okay. The man led them up three flights of stairs, down a narrow dilapidated hall, and into a cramped apartment. There were three others inside: two young men and a woman, the first Miller had seen not covering her face.

"This is the one?" the woman asked in English. Auzhan nodded. Slowly, Miller removed the headscarf.

Although they were obviously disturbed by him, Auzhan's associates tried their best not to show it. The woman nodded and then spoke to one of the young men in Kurdish. "Miller, right? Sit. We'll get you food, then you need to sleep."

"We've radioed our friend," said the older gentlemen who'd led them in, "He says there will be a trawler waiting for you just before dawn. They'll take you to Ras al-Khaimah, and from there you can arrange for passage to Dubai, Abu Dhabi, or wherever else you want."

The young man returns from the kitchen with some reheated leftovers: rice mixed with raisins, fish, and onions. Miller digs in voraciously, having forgotten just how hungry he was. When he finished, he nodded politely, then asked:

"Why are you helping me?"

"That isn't quite as important as who you are and why you are here," the woman replied.

"Sabouri knows all that already. Didn't he tell you?"

"I did," said Auzhan, taking the seat across from Miller, "But my interrogation isn't yet finished." Auzhan smiles, but Miller looks horrified. "I want to know about your future. You are an American astronaut. Who else besides America has ships such as the one that crashed in your time?"

Miller is reluctant to answer: "All of the great powers do... America, India, Turkestan, the Union..."

"And Iran?"

Miller hesitates. "Iran doesn't exist anymore." Auzhan frowns, but lets him continue: "Most of the countries that exist in your time don't exist 400 years from now."

"Yet, America survives. Typical," says the woman, rolling her eyes. Auzhan leans closer. Miller freezes, as a gazelle might when it realizes that it's been spotted by a hungry cheetah.

"In Kerman, you said that I must 'survive' to become President," he whispered, "Why?"

"Why what?" replied Miller quietly.

"What must I survive?" asked Auzhan, but Miller does not immediately answer. "Something is about to happen isn't it?" Miller shook his head.

"No..."

"What is it, Miller? Is it a disaster? A war?" Auzhan prodded, "What must we survive?"

"I can't..."

Auzhan grabbed Miller and shouted:

"Is this the reason why Iran doesn't exist in your time? What is coming? Tell us!"

"Even if I tell you, you can't stop it!" Miller shouted back, his voice nearly cracking, "If it could be stopped, if it were possible to go back in time and change something, it wouldn't have happened in the first place! My future wouldn't exist!"

"We can still try..."

"And you'll fail! You have to!"

"I don't HAVE to do anything," Auzhan hissed, letting him go, "But I will do whatever it takes to save this country from every enemy, foreign... and domestic." Auzhan leaned in close again and whispered: "What happened?"

"It was..." Miller paused, still reluctant. "The war. The third one."

"With who? What war?" asked Auzhan, "A third Gulf war?"

"No," said Miller, "World War."

Auzhan pulled away from Miller as if he were Satan himself. The woman and older gentlemen looked horrified.

"How...?" Auzhan managed to say.

"I... I don't really remember. It's been a long time since I read about it," Miller replied, "Something about a nuclear exchange in the middle east that spread to India and China."

"When?" asked Auzhan.

"Soon, I guess. It was at the beginning of the 21st century, at the end of something called the Terror War. Or was it the September War?" Miller explained, "America was fighting in Mesopotamia against guerillas, but it wasn't America or the guerillas who started it. The theory was that Iran attacked Israel for some reason, and then it all just went on from there..." Auzhan paled and then looked to the others.

"You don't suppose..."

"It's impossible," replied the older gentlemen, "It can't fail."

"But what would happen if it did?" asked the woman.

"The government would be pissed, that's what," Auzhan answered, "And then they'd move against the obvious culprit."

Miller tried to follow the sudden conversation in Farsi, but got nowhere and remained utterly confused. "What is it?"

Auzhan ignored Miller: "We have to abort."

"No!" shouted the older gentlemen, "We're too far along. It was hard enough to get someone on the inside to help us... we may not get another chance like this!"

"Don't you get it? It's NOT going to work!" Auzhan shouted back.

"You don't know that!" yelled the old man.

"It's fucking OBVIOUS!" Auzhan roared in English as he stood, "I don't know how, I don't know why, but the bomb isn't going to work! The Supreme Leader, or the President, or maybe even both are going to survive! And guess who WE have all set up to take the fall for the attempt? ISRAEL. And what is the survivor going to do about it? ATTACK. And you heard for yourself what happens after that!"

"Wait, what?!" said Miller. He looked at Auzhan, stunned and confused. It was like learning that Lyndon Johnson had arranged the assassination of Martin Luther King, but still went on to push through the Civil Rights Act.

Again, Auzhan ignored him: "I want to free our country from the Mullahs, but not like this. I'm not going to be responsible for unleashing armageddon."

Tires screeched outside. The woman turned to the window.

"It's VEVAK!" she cursed, "Dammit! You led them right to us!"

"We must leave, now!" said Auzhan, pulling his gun from its holster. Everyone ran into the hall. Shouts and heavy footsteps could be heard in the stairwell heading to the front door.

"This way!" said the old man. They ran to the other end of the hall and a second stairwell. Gunshots blared, barely missing Miller as he ducked through. The old man wasn't so lucky. Miller stopped, frozen by the man's empty eyes.

"Go! Don't stop! Go!" shouted Auzhan, grabbing Miller and shoving him forward. More shots, slamming into the stairs behind them. Auzhan fires back, but doesn't hit anything. They reach the bottom of the stairwell. The young man kicks the door open and they rush out the back door.

"Hurry! This way!" he said, running toward a beat up brown van. He pulls a set of keys from his pocket... before falling in a hail of bullets. Auzhan, Miller, and the woman dive to the ground. Auzhan fires back, hitting one of the VEVAK agents while the others duck back into the tenement. The woman grabs the keys from the boy's limp fingers and they run for the van.

The three leapt into the van, Miller diving in the back while the woman took the wheel. The van kicked up dirt and gravel as they sped off. Auzhan fired his pistol out the passenger's side window, gunning down a VEVAK agent as they roared past the tenements and onto the road, others firing after them. The back window shattered. Soon, they were beyond the range of the guns.

"Did we make it?" asked Miller, "Are they following

us?"

Suddenly, an SUV shot out of a side street and screeched to a halt in the middle of the road. The windows opened and the VEVAK agents inside fired.

"Get down!" shouted Auzhan. Bullets slammed into the van. The woman was killed instantly, reduced to a bloody mess. Something in the engine was hit, spewing a smoky plume. The van veered to the side, rolled across the sidewalk, through the guard railing, and finally slammed into the Persian Gulf. The VEVAK agents ran to the sea's edge, their guns raised, but found only blood and oil seeping from the van as it slipped below the blackened waves.

One of the agents spoke into a radio: "Team three to command: the suspects have neutralized, but the package has also been lost. Send in the clean-up crew."

As the men turned away, none noticed a shadow in the dark water – half swimming, half carried by the tide. The figure, not quite recovered from the crash, stayed as silent and still as possible while making his inexorable escape, barely breathing even after the voices, radio static, cars, and helicopters have vanished into the shadowy horizon. Finally, shivering and battered, he swam ashore, crawling onto the sand in a daze. He flopped over and stared up at the moon.

After a long while, Miller finally gasped: "What am I supposed to do now?"

My First Fake

I remember the first time I ever saw a Fake.

"It's just a dog," I'd said, "A golden retriever. What's so special about that?" I was eleven, and the teachers had huddled all of us together in the gym – nothing new, they liked to force the kids to sit through hour-long speeches about computer addiction or fire safety...but this was different. I'm not sure who figured it out first, but the whispers spread fast through the crowd:

"A Fake! A Fake! It's a Fake!"

I was transfixed. A Fake? It couldn't be! It looked so real, so normal! A little man in a gray jacket was also on the stage, giving some rehearsed speech to the student body, introducing us to this new era of human history. What did he say? I can't remember anymore, but one bit stuck out:

"This is Pascal. She's not a real dog, but a fake one made out of millions and millions of microscopic machines. Say hello to everyone, Pascal!"

Ever since then, I've been amazed by Fakes. Like all other technologies, improvements came soon after: intelligent AI, language, more and more complicated forms. Every dazzling innovation just made the Fakes seem more and more miraculous in my mind: as if mankind had finally found a way to make every fantastic element of our imaginations reality. Of all the great breakthroughs of the last sixty years, nothing surpasses the Fakes. They are, in my opinion at least, humanity's greatest achievement.

Fifteen years later, I was a few years out of college and working a vaguely interesting job at an accounting firm in Atlanta. It was tedious work, little more than typing numbers over and over again, but at least I could afford to start paying off my student loans. At around two in the afternoon, one of my co-workers, an older fellow with graying hair and a thick brown mustache, appeared in my cubicle door.

"Hey," John asked, "You like Fakes, right?"

I glanced at him for a moment before typing in the next line of numbers.

"Yeah. Why?"

"Well, you see," he said in the usual southern drawl, "My son is selling his Fake and wants to use the money to help buy a new car. You know how kids are. So, being that you're a big Fake fanatic and all..." I was surprised... I thought I'd kept my interest in Fakes quiet.

"...I was wondering if you would mind taking a look at it."

To be honest, the offer made me feel giddy, like a kid on Christmas morning. The words "Oh Wow! My first Fake!" kept repeating in my head, over and over. Fakes had recently become affordable enough for the average person to buy, but being so deep in debt I hadn't seriously considered trying to get one. I tried to restrain myself from accepting outright, but John had already seen my eyes light up.

His smile erased any doubts. "How about tonight? Would eight be good for you?"

"Oh, yeah, sure."

John lived in a smallish one-family house in a quiet neighborhood on the far side of town. He greeted me at the door with a big, friendly smile, led me into an understandably messy living room, and introduced me to his wife and two kids.

"Want something to eat?" he asked, "We just finished dinner."

"No, thanks," I replied, before looking around expectantly, "So...ah...where is...?" I must've been bouncing up and down with excitement, because the smile John gave me was so big, he must have been holding back laughter.

"Okay, okay," he said, before turning and giving a loud call, "Junior!" John's oldest son, a teenager around seventeen or eighteen, walked in from the kitchen. "This is the guy from work I was telling you about. He wants to see

Satoshi, so why don't you take him around back and let him take a look?"

"Sure, dad."

Junior led me into their pristine, well-manicured backyard. I almost tripped over a bike left in the middle of the lawn before we reached a large shed nestled in a back corner among a few hedges and flower bushes. That's when I started to feel uneasy, even more so when Junior reached into his pocket and pulled out a key. The shed's door was padlocked. I tried shoving the terrible thoughts from my mind, reminding myself that John was a good man, with a good family. The door swung open, and the stench of gasoline and fertilizer poured into my face. Junior entered, and I followed.

The interior was dark and humid, a putrid odor hanging in the still, stale air. The only sound I could hear was our own shallow breathing as Junior fumbled along the wall searching for the light switch. I heard the quiet sound of metal scratching on concrete moments before the searing florescent light sliced through the dark, and for that brief moment before my eyes readjusted to the light, I had hoped that I had gone blind. Then, I saw Satoshi.

His first reaction was to leap at me with his jaws wide and fangs bare. There was a feral look in his eyes...an intense hatred that I had never seen before. I gasped, tripping backwards as the creature attacked. Without warning, he stopped in midair and flung away, smacking into the shed's back wall with a loud thud. I caught my breath as Junior laughed, and Satoshi shot the most frightening glare I've ever seen at us both. I clambered to my feet as my mind raced to take in what was happening.

"Oh! He got the jump on you!" the teen laughed, "Nasty bastard, ain't he? He's pretty vicious, so we got an E-Collar to keep him tied down." Satoshi growled a reply, letting his feeling on the matter be known, although I doubt Junior noticed. As he started to go on and on about how "bad ass" Satoshi was, and how "cool" his hobby, "Fake Fighting", was, I couldn't help but stare at the miserable wreck laying in front of me. Satoshi was a Myth-Type Fake, a Fake designed to take on the appearance of some fantastic animal from mythology. In this case, Satoshi's genome had been designed to resemble a dinosaur or dragon of some kind. His scales had a dark red tint, although it was hard to tell with that layer of grime and dried internal fluid covering it. I stared, and he just glared back with a hatred that I will never be able to fathom. After what seemed like an eternity, I blinked and turned away. I couldn't bear to look at him.

"How... how much do you... want for him?" I finally managed to bark. Junior paused for a moment, although I wasn't sure if he was thinking of a price or surprised that I wanted Satoshi at all.

"Five hundred sounds good to me," he replied. I fished out my wallet and handed him the cash. It wiped out last week's paycheck but... for this, it was worth it. After that, I silently walked back into John's yard and held back a desperate urge to scream. I could barely contain my disgust for what I'd just seen, the outright disregard for simple dignity. I took a deep breath, but it did little to help. After Junior wrestled Satoshi into a cage and stuffed him in my car's back seat, I quickly bid John good night and got out of there.

I drove in a daze. I had just discovered one of those simple dark truths about a guy I otherwise had no problem with. I also had an abused Fake cramped into a cage in my back seat. What the hell happened? It was supposed to be a good and happy day, not a god damned nightmare! As I stopped at a red light, I realized a few more tidbits: it was raining, I'd been driving for just under two hours, and I was lost.

"Fuck!" I shouted, slamming the steering wheel and startling Satoshi, who I heard jump inside the cage. I sighed and looked at the cage through my rear view mirror. "Satoshi... I'm sorry. I'm sorry for everything that asshole did to you. I... god, I must sound like an idiot. Why the hell should you even give a damn about anything I say? Just... I don't know. I don't know what to do. I always wanted a Fake. Maybe it was because I didn't have many friends as a kid, but all I know is that this was always my dream. Funny..." The light turned green and I stopped talking. He probably wasn't even listening anyway. After a while, though, I finally muttered one more thing:

"I'm sorry. I should have ripped that fucktard's throat out myself."

Thirty Years Away

"Do you think this is...unfair?"

Cecilia squinted and tilted her head.

"What is?"

I leaned back in my seat – at a table in front of the Plaza Café on 33rd street – and bit into a pistachio cookie. The day was nice, relaxed, a good day to just talk over coffee between classes.

"Everything. The mission, I mean."

"What?" she said and stirred sweetener into her latte. "Of course not, I think it's kind of an honor. The whole world thought our parents were worthy of representing all of humanity..."

"That's my point," I said. "We had no say in the decision. Most of our parents aren't going to live long enough to finish the mission. Hell, a good chunk of our generation won't be around in thirty years either."

Cecilia shrugged.

"That's nature of interstellar spaceflight..."

"I understand that, I get that this is the only way it could happen: stuff a city's worth of people into a spaceship, shoot them toward the stars and pray the later generations do what you sent them to. I'm just..."

"Resentful?"

I sighed again and my eyes wandered. A TV in the video store across the street was flashing the latest Hollywood blockbuster – latest for us, but in reality a decade old.

"You know me. I teach my students about so many places they and I won't ever see...Paris, New York, Africa, Fiji...I'll never get the chance to set foot on Earth. Maybe my grandkids will someday, but not me."

Cecilia sipped and licked sand-colored foam from her lips. "You don't want to be here?"

"I probably would've turned down the offer, Earth is interesting enough."

Cecilia looked up: lazy whips of vapor below a digital blue sky.

"I'm sure I would have said yes," she said. "Earth may be interesting, but there's a whole new world out there, full of people, places, and things waiting to be seen and experienced." She sighed and ran a finger over her latte's paper brim. "Thinking about it, though...this is pretty unfair to the Gliesians, isn't it?"

I nodded and finished my last cookie.

"Just think," she continued. "The message from Gliese 581 came only fifteen years before we started the voyage. By the time the Gliesians were told that Earth was sending an expedition, we were a third of the way there."

"Way too late to say no," I said and sighed. "They weren't given a choice either."

"I want to go, I want to meet them, it just doesn't seem right that we started this trip uninvited."

"It reminds me of the American Pilgrims – you've heard of them, right? How they set off to colonize the New World. They sought religious freedom, but in achieving it they imposed their own values on the aboriginal Americans..." I said.

Cecilia looked glum while she nodded.

"And the native population was destroyed."

"Um...yes."

I stirred my coffee.

"We shouldn't get ahead of ourselves. The situations aren't really the same. First, we know the history. We know not to repeat those mistakes and, second, the Gliesians know we're coming...well, now they do at least. Lastly, we're not going to colonize their world, just the one next door. We have their permission, so it's not like we're invading their solar system."

Cecilia shook her head. "The way I see it, that doesn't really mean much. Of course they're going to tell us it is okay: we're the ones advanced enough to make this trip. They aren't."

"Do you think they're afraid of us?"

"I wouldn't be surprised.   We haven't threatened them, but our aggressive behavior must be frightening," she said. "Our intentions are good – at least I hope they are. Maybe trade will be enough to make up for it."

I glanced at my watch.   "We should probably be heading back."

Campus was only a couple blocks away. On the way, we passed by a bus stop, a faded poster glued to the side boasted:

"Gliese 581: Only Thirty Years Away!"

Cecilia and I sighed.

Doravon vs. Raynor

"Raynor?" Laurie whispered, gently touching her elder brother's shoulder, "Are you okay? You've been quiet for a long time now." He glanced back with those crystal blue eyes of his, and smiled.

"I'm fine," he said, "My mind just wandered off."

"I'm scared, Raynor. I have such a horrible feeling…"

"Don't worry. These doctors know what they're talking about. I trust them. After this, we can go home and get on with our lives as if none of this ever happened," he replied. Really, he's just as afraid and worried as his sister, but he couldn't show that to her. He wouldn't worry her any more than he already has.

This sickness…no, this curse, has destroyed their lives. All of their friends and relatives have been driven away.

This trip, this treatment, and these doctors are their final hope. The doctors claimed they could cure him, free him of this curse, and give back his life.

In his mind, Raynor prayed, "I hope so."

The office was blazing white, little in the way of personal affects besides a photo or two on the desk. Raynor James shook hands with Dr. Immanuel Lorelei, the man who first approached and told him about this place.

"Mr. James, I'm glad you could make it," he said, "Welcome to United Medical. Please, both of you, take a seat." They do so as Dr. Lorelei eases back into his leather chair. "Raynor, you have a very unique condition. Studies show that your disease is contracted by less than one percent of the entire human population. In truth, you're the first proven case of Physical Lycanthropy in recent history. This treatment is purely experimental in nature, but if successful, not only will you be cured, we will have a fundamental understanding of the disease and a precedent for treatment."

"I see…"

"Is it really safe?" asks Laurie, "Are you sure that this is a safe procedure?"

"As I said, this treatment is still experimental, so there's always the chance of an accident," Dr. Lorelei replies, smiling reassuringly, "But, I assure you, we're taking every precaution."

"Okay…" Laurie sighs, her worries still not entirely vanquished. She turns to her brother, the one symbol of hope and strength in her life, and smiles. She wants the treatment to succeed…but can't shake this cold, foreboding feeling hanging over her. Her heart wants to proceed, but something even deeper is screaming to stop. Laurie does not listen.

A group of men in white lab coats escort Raynor to a small observation room and give him a quick physical. After a short while, Dr. Lorelei enters, followed by another scientist.

"Where's Laurie?" Raynor immediately asks.

"Outside. We don't want her to be in here...just in case," the doctor replies, taking a syringe from one of the scientists, "Inside this syringe is a genetically engineered retrovirus, designed specifically to carry genetic material and insert it into your DNA."

"So...you plan to cure me by replacing the infected genes?" asks Raynor, already having a basic understanding of gene therapy, "Will that work?"

"Theoretically," Lorelei replies, "But, the only way to truly know is to try it." Raynor smiles courageously.

"Let's do it."

Dr. Lorelei raises Raynor's sleeve, applies some alcohol, and then gently stabs the metal needle into the young man's arm. Raynor shuts his eyes tightly as the liquid is injected, the sensation none-to-pleasing. Finally, Lorelei pulls the syringe away.

"Now, keep in mind, you aren't likely to see any immediate effects and you're probably going to need multiple treatments over the course of..."

"RAARGH!!"

Lorelei is suddenly interrupted as Raynor begins roaring at the top of his lungs. It quickly becomes apparent why: his body has begun to change. He is growing…morphing into a werewolf! Lorelei falls to the ground and quickly crawls backwards, away from Raynor.

"What's happening?!" screams one of the aides.

"I…I don't know! It's two in the afternoon…this shouldn't be…" Dr. Lorelei stammers, "Unless…the gene! That damned retrovirus must have dropped the gene in the wrong spot! It's cause a chain reaction in his DNA…!"

Raynor roars again as his bulging muscles tear his clothes to shreds. Long, black hair sprouts along his entire body while ivory white fangs appear in his jaws. His hands turn into claws, his ears grow long and pointed, and a tail becomes clearly visible. All the while, he keeps growing. Bigger, and bigger, and even bigger still.

The United Medical facility rumbles thunderously as the still-growing beast bursts out of its prison, tossing huge slabs of concrete and metal about. As the creature finally stands its immense full height, it squints. It's eyes are virgin to the bright afternoon sunlight. The beast scans the concrete and verdant terrain. It sniffs the air, detecting the salty breeze blowing from the ocean miles away and the sweet smell of living flesh. Prey. With boundless vigor, the wolf-monster springs across the roof, leaps to the ground below, and dashes off into the distance.

"Raynor! Raynor!!" screams Laurie, running out of the building along with Dr. Lorelei and dozens of white-coats, "Brother!" He does not stop. Suddenly, she spins around, a fiery rage burning in her eyes as she grabs Lorelei by the collar of his shirt.

"What did you DO to him?!" Laurie growls angrily.

"The...the gene..." the scientist fearfully stammers, "It...it landed in...the wrong spot."

"What the hell does that mean?"

"It means that your brother's DNA has gone out of control," one of the scientists explains, "Instead of curing him, our therapy has transformed him into an even greater threat than he was before. Ms. James, your brother is dead, murdered by his own inner demon."

Laurie drops Lorelei as she replies, "Then you undo the therapy. Put him back to the way he was before!"

"We can't!" Lorelei shouts back, "The treatment is irreversible." Laurie scans the apologetic faces staring at her only once before turning to look in the direction her brother had run off in, dozens of conflicting thoughts and feelings racing through her mind.

"Raynor..."

- - -

Meanwhile, only a few short miles away, another beastly predator is stalking its own prey. He purrs with anticipation, razor sharp claws digging into the soft soil as he eyes a crowd of Parasauropholus meandering about the watering hole. The predator shifts his weight a bit before finally choosing a specific target: a meaty male with a slight limp. Suddenly, someone trumpets a warning cry. The predator smirks. Now the fun begins!

Like a bullet, the predator, a Tyrannosaurus-like monster called "Doravon", plows out from behind the tree-line and charges towards the herd. The Parasauropholus have been slow to react to the warning, only now beginning to stampede away. They quickly realize that there is no chance of escape, though, when a second Doravon, this one female, cuts them off. She tears into one, the Matriarch as it turns out, blood spraying in all directions, as the huntress crushes the Matriarch's neck and tosses her limp corpse aside. With their herd's leader dead, the Parasauropholus lose all resolve flee in all directions.

Her own prey caught, the huntress looks over at her mate, just in time to watch him pounce on a limping straggler. At first, it seems as if the predator has made an egregious error: his claws sink in the Parasauropholus' side with such force that it sends both rolling head-over-heels into the watering hole. Dirt, blood, and water splash everywhere as the pair thrash about violently. Someone screams. Finally, all is silent as Doravon rises from the crimson waters, the prey hanging limply in his jaws. The huntress, ever amused by her mate's antics, smiles in her mind. What a water bug!

Doravon and the huntress have been bonded for a little less than a year now. There had always been an attraction between them, even when they were just hatchlings. Back then, the huntress always loved to play with the silly male for hours and hours. As they grew older, she grew to admire his courage and skill as a hunter and fighter. When it came time to choose a mate, he became the obvious choice. As you might imagine, their courtship was extremely short.

Having eaten their fill, the couple leisurely strolls back

towards their nest. Under normal circumstances it would be a sign of absolute idiocy for them to both go hunting and leave their clutch of eggs unguarded. But, they are different. Ever since the Huntress laid her eggs, their nest has been watched over at all hours of the day by shiny buzzing birds. Whenever any threat approaches the nest, these birds swoop down and scare it away. Thanks to this special protection, Doravon and the huntress have been able to continue hunting together as a team.

Doravon purrs, rubbing his face against his mate's neck affectionately. Suddenly, she stops. Confused, he sniffs the air and picks up an unfamiliar scent...filthy and sweaty is the only way his mind can decipher it. Then he realizes: he can't hear the buzzing birds. His heart skips a beat. The nest! The pair sprint the rest of the way home.

The sight that greets them is utterly horrifying: the smashed and burning corpse of a buzzing bird, the blood and yolk covered ruins of the nest, and, worst of all, the monstrous culprit. The beast growls at them, watching with ravenous, feral eyes. Enraged, the huntress roars and then leaps at the monster, who raises an arm in defense. The huntress' fangs sink in the creature's forearm, but it gives no thought as it tears her off itself and tosses the dinosaur aside. Another roar and Doravon rams his forehead into the beast's gut. The huntress then pounces on the beast's hairy back before taking another vicious bite into the monster's shoulder. It howls, not in pain, but anger.

The black-furred beast wraps its claws around the huntress' neck and flips her towards Doravon, who is just barely to avoid being struck himself. Unfortunately, he isn't fast enough to dodge a second attack. With amazing speed, the beast charges at the dinosaur and delivers a powerful right hook, sending Doravon flying through a nearby tree, which shatters into splinters.

Painfully, the huntress, her body sore and bloodied, regains her footing. Seeing that her mate has been knocked into a barely conscious daze, she growls fiercely at murderous intruder and charges yet again. The monster breaks into a sadistic sneer, then leaps at the huntress, catching her throat in his fearsome jaws and lifting her off of the ground. She struggles, kicking at the beast and thrashing her tail, but the lupine creature is unfazed. It bites tighter. The huntress gasps, her eyes glaze over, and her body goes limp. The murderer drops her corpse.

Doravon watches all of this, helpless to save his mate. He watches the monster stare at her corpse with a familiar expression: the look one gives when considering whether or not to actually eat one's kill.

Helpless.

A voice. Small, shrill – a little creature emerges from the forest, quickly followed by a pack of others carry black sticks and other strange things.

Ray-nor, it said.

The beast seemed frozen, entranced by this single insignificant figure. It stepped toward him, yapping away soft sounds – the monster's ears twitched, some sort of recognition, a softening of the face…

Doravon's tired and blurred eyes wandered, settling on the still form of the Huntress.

Rage.

Everything screaming, Doravon rose, roared, and ran. Startled, the beast didn't run, couldn't run – just stare wide -eyed as Doravon clamped his jaws on the bastard's throat. Doravon barreled ahead, driving the squirming, bleeding beast into a tree. For a second, their eyes meet. For an entire second, Doravon glares into those eyes, pumping all of his hatred and fury and despair into them.

The predator shoved his foot into the murderous wolf's chest and pulled back, tearing it's throat out. The killer fell with a thud. It died moments later.

Doravon roared, but he felt no relief, closure or victory.

There was only sorrow.

About the Author

A writer for as far back as he could remember, Paul V. Cwiakala was raised on a steady diet of Science Fiction, Fantasy, and Adventure movies ranging from novels by Harry Turtledove and H. G. Wells to movies written by Shinichi Sekizawa and Lawrence Kasdan. Having written short stories throughout his youth, Paul wrote his first novel while pursuing undergraduate studies at William Paterson University, where he earned a Bachelor's Degree in Communications in 2009.

Paul published his first novel, *Fallen Saints*, through Silk Baron Independent Press in 2014. His second book, *A Slave of the Bird Men*, was published in 2016.

Also Available From
Silk Baron Independent Press

FALLEN SAINTS

AN ANCIENT RELIC. POWERFUL FANATICS.
A WOMAN AND HER GUN.

Two thousand years ago, the Power of God and the ability to perform powerful magic were revealed to the world. Protected by the Church, only the powerful magic-wielding "Miracle Workers" today know these divine secrets.

Now, in an American Old West where gunslingers and magic are facts of everyday life, Angie Grissom and her Cajun partner, Andrew Carnation, hunt down criminals for cash with little more than their wits and brawn. But when the hunt for a simple thief puts her in the middle of a religious blood feud between two factions of fanatical Miracle Workers and a battle over an ancient book with ties to the very origin of their powers, will Angie's quick draw be enough?

Action and adventure await in a Wild West that never was!

A SLAVE OF THE
BIRD MEN

A SAILOR LEFT FOR DEAD
IN A LAND WHERE BIRDS RULE!

Francisco del Puerto had dreams of gold and adventure when he joined an expedition to explore the far-off Americas. But, after a fateful encounter on the shores of the Rio De La Plata he's been left stranded and at the mercy of the Bird Men—a race of intelligent birds inhabiting a South America very different from the one history knew. Taken as a slave by the enigmatic Lord Ereter, can Francisco learn to live and survive among them in this strange new world?

Adventure and Survival in a South America that never was!